Ready, Set, Go!

by
Robert Munsch

illustrated by
Michael Martchenko

Scholastic Canada Ltd.
New York Toronto London Auckland Sydney
Mexico City New Delhi Hong Kong Buenos Aires

Scholastic Canada Ltd.
604 King Street West, Toronto, Ontario M5V 1E1, Canada

Scholastic Inc.
557 Broadway, New York, NY 10012, USA

Scholastic Australia Pty Limited
PO Box 579, Gosford, NSW 2250, Australia

Scholastic New Zealand Limited
Private Bag 94407, Botany, Manukau 2163, New Zealand

Scholastic Children's Books
Euston House, 24 Eversholt Street, London NW1 1DB, UK

www.scholastic.ca

The illustrations in this book were painted in watercolour
on Crescent illustration board.
The type is set in 26 point Goudy Modern.

Library and Archives Canada Cataloguing in Publication

Munsch, Robert N., 1945-, author
Ready, set, go! / Robert Munsch ; illustrated by Michael
Martchenko.

ISBN 978-1-4431-4658-6 (pbk.)

I. Martchenko, Michael, illustrator II. Title.

PS8576.U575R43 2015b   jC813'.54   C2015-902509-5

6 5 4 3 2 1   Printed in Canada 114   15 16 17 18 19

For Miranda Lee,
Vancouver, British Columbia.
— R.M.

Before her father's big race, Miranda and her dad went out for breakfast. Miranda had eggs and waffles and fruit and a whole pitcher of orange juice.

Then they were late for the race because Miranda had to stop five times to go to the bathroom.

When they got there, her dad jumped out of the car and yelled, "Miranda! I have to go sign up for the race. Hurry and get me some water. If I don't drink something before the race starts I'll never finish."

So Miranda went looking for a bottle of water.

Suddenly the starting horn went off and the race was on.

"Oh no!" said Miranda. "He has to get some water or he will never win."

She found a bottle of water and ran up the road looking for her father.

The first person she saw was walking. His face was green and he looked like he was going to fall over. Miranda decided not to ask him if he had seen her dad. She just kept going.

Miranda caught up to the next runner. He was a regular sort of runner and was not green at all.

Miranda said, "Have you seen my dad? His name is Peter."

"Go away, kid," said the man. "Pipsqueaks don't belong in this race."

So Miranda kept going.

Miranda caught up to the next runner. She said, "Have you seen my dad? His name is Peter."

"Get out of my way, kid," said the woman. "Pipsqueaks don't belong in this race."

"Well, I'm faster than you," said Miranda, and she ran ahead and left the woman behind.

Miranda passed runners in pink tutus, jugglers and people dressed as carrots, but none of them had seen her dad.

17

She ran up hills and down hills,
past stores and fire stations and
crowds of people waving signs,
but nobody had seen her dad.

There were 200 people ahead of her. Some were nice to her and some didn't answer and some called her a pipsqueak, but none of them had seen her dad.

Finally Miranda came to a man who was running very fast.

"Have you seen my dad?" she said. "His name is Peter."

"Oh no!" yelled the man. "Is he ahead of me? I thought I was first."

"Wow," said Miranda, "my dad is winning and he didn't even get his drink of water."

Finally she came to the finish line, but she still didn't see her father. Suddenly a bunch of people grabbed her and lifted her up into the air.

They cheered, "She wins! The little pipsqueak wins!" and they would not put her down.

Miranda yelled, "Has anybody seen my dad? His name is Peter."

All of a sudden her dad was right in front of her.

"Where were you?" said Miranda. "I was looking for you all over. Here is your water."

"Thanks," said her dad. "I was late starting. I didn't even finish the race. I hear a little kid won. Did you see her?"